The Bearden Foundation would like to thank Robin D. G. Kelley, who made this book possible.

SIMON & SCHUSTER BOOKS FOR YOUNG READERS
An imprint of Simon & Schuster Children's Publishing Division
1230 Avenue of the Americas, New York, New York 10020
Copyright © 2003 by Romare Bearden Foundation/Licensed by **VAGA**, New York, NY
Foreword copyright © 2003 by Henry Louis Gates Jr.
SIMON & SCHUSTER BOOKS FOR YOUNG READERS is a trademark of Simon & Schuster.
Book design by Dan Potash
The text for this book is set in Egyptian 710.
The illustrations for this book are rendered in mixed media.
Manufactured in China
2 4 6 8 10 9 7 5 3 1

Library of Congress Cataloging-in-Publication Data
Bearden, Romare, 1911-1988.
Li'l Dan, the drummer boy : a Civil War story / Romare Bearden.
p. cm.
Summary: When a company of black Union soldiers tells Li'l Dan that he is no longer a slave,
he follows them, and uses his beloved drum to save them from attack.
ISBN 0-689-86237-7 (hardcover)
1. United States—History—Civil War, 1861–1865—Juvenile fiction.
[1. United States—History—Civil War, 1861–1865—Fiction.
2. African Americans—Fiction. 3. Drums—Fiction.] I. Title.
PZ7.B38026Li 2003
[E]—dc21
2003003548

The original artwork by Romare Bearden, completed in 1983,
is published here for the first time.

LI'L DAN
the drummer boy

A CIVIL WAR STORY

Romare Bearden

Foreword by Henry Louis Gates Jr.

Simon & Schuster Books for Young Readers
New York   London   Toronto   Sydney   Singapore

FOREWORD

Spending time with the great artist Romare Bearden and learning about Li'l Dan, the drummer boy hero of his wonderful book, are among the highlights of my life. Back in the late 1970s, when I was a professor at Yale University, I would often take the train from New Haven, Connecticut, to New York, and spend Saturday afternoons with Bearden and the writer and critic Albert Murray. In those days, "Romie," as his friends called him, was finally enjoying wide critical acclaim after laboring as an artist for nearly four decades. He was completing a series of collages of jazz musicians that would become some of his best-known work, and his stature and influence were greater than that of any other African-American artist before him. The three of us usually began the day at Books & Company on Madison Avenue, where we scoured the shelves for works of fiction, criticism, philosophy, art, and music. Bearden, a large, eloquent, light-skinned man with a big round head that always reminded me of former Soviet leader Nikita Khrushchev, had an insatiable appetite for books and an awesome intellect. He would typically pick up a copy of something daunting like R. M. Rilke's *Letters on Cezanne* and insist that I read it on the train back to New Haven that night.

After a couple of hours in the bookstore, perusing, reflecting, discussing, and eventually buying, we'd head next door to the Madison Café, where Romie always ordered the same thing: the largest fruit salad that I had ever seen in public. Although he claimed that dietary considerations informed his choice, I was convinced that he ordered the fruit salad in order to devour the colors, like an artist dipping his brush into his palette. He'd start laying the ground with the off-white of the apples and the bananas, and follow them with the pinkish orange of the grapefruit, the red of strawberries, the speckled green of kiwifruit; the blueberries and purple grapes he'd save for last. He had a master's eye, for sure, but he also had a kid's fascination with color and all of its magical qualities.

One Saturday after one of those great lunches, we headed downtown to Romie's loft at 357 Canal Street and continued our conversation. He showed me some of his work and then suddenly asked me if I wanted to come see his studio in Long Island City. After we arrived, he sat me down and began pulling out a stack of beautiful panels he'd been working on to illustrate the story of "a little drummer boy during the Civil War." He carefully laid the first picture on the floor and began narrating the tale that accompanied it. Then he laid down the next image, and the next, each time telling more of the story that had been percolating in his head. By the time he had come to the end of the story, the floor was covered with these absolutely stunning, colorful panels, and I was in awe. "So what do you think?" Romie asked. "It's marvelous!" I told him. Every time I saw him after that, I'd ask about the book and encourage him to write it and publish it.

That Saturday in Long Island City was truly one of the most beautiful days in my life. What a privilege it was to see Romie's magnificent illustrations and to hear his wonderful story in his own voice. And it is a privilege now to introduce this book to the world, all these years later. Although he wrote *Li'l Dan, the Drummer Boy* over two decades ago, Bearden's poignant and compelling tale will resonate with readers from every generation and every background. Perhaps the main lesson of the book might be read as an unintentional revelation about its author, for it shows what one person can do with a few creative tools, profound ingenuity, and a deep and abiding love for one's art, our common history, and our shared humanity

Henry Louis Gates Jr.
Cambridge, Massachusetts
September 2003

The workday was long and hard for slaves on cotton plantations. When the cotton was high, everyone was in the fields picking and baling it from sunup to sundown.

On the Hollis plantation, when the day's work was over, Li'l Dan always came to listen to Mr. Ned play his drum. Mr. Ned said that his father had given him the drum and taught him how to play it. He said, "This drum came from a faraway place called Africa, way across the water."

And each day Mr. Ned taught Li'l Dan drumming, just the way he had learned from his father.

One Sunday, Dan borrowed an ax and went in the woods, where he worked all day making his own drum. When he finished, Dan stretched a pig hide over the top and pulled it taut with the heavy twine used to bind the cotton bales.

When he showed the drum to Mr. Ned, the old man said, "Dan, you done fine. You got a real good drum there."

Dan tried to imitate all the sounds he heard around him. The rhythm of people singing. The cawing of the birds. The clacking of the leaves as they were fanned by a passing wind.

Dan even stayed out in the rain to catch the pattern of rain and the heavy crash of thunder.

One day Dan noticed there was hardly anyone in the fields, and he heard a loud galloping noise down on the main road. Maybe, he thought, this was something to play on the drum.

Suddenly a long line of horsemen in gray uniforms swept down the road through clouds of brown dust.

Soon after the strange horsemen passed, people from the plantation appeared, scurrying along the road with bundles on their backs.

Dan ran up to the big house where the "master" lived and found many black men in blue uniforms. *What could have happened?* Dan wondered.

One of the men in uniform, whom Dan heard some of the other men call "captain," came over to Dan. "What is your name, little boy?" he asked.

Dan said, "My name is Dan."

"Where are your mother and father?"

Dan said, "I hear tell they were sold away when I was most young. I just belong here."

"Well, son," said the captain, "you don't belong here anymore. You're free now."

Dan asked, "What do that mean?"

"It means you can go anywhere you like. We've been fighting a civil war against the Southern slave masters, the 'rebels,' for over three years—since 1861. Last year President Lincoln declared all slaves free. The rebels don't want slavery to end so they keep fighting. But we just beat them back. Many of these soldiers were slaves just like you. Now they're fighting for freedom."

Now Dan was confused. If he could only find **Mr. Ned!** After the soldiers gave him some food, he decided to follow them as they marched away. Somewhere along the way he might see **Mr. Ned.**

he soldiers came to know Li'l Dan. One of them, named Scipio, said he had a little boy the same age as Dan. Scipio said, "One day I'm going back to where I came from and find him."

The soldiers came to a place where a large engine was waiting, snorting steam and thunder. It reminded Dan of the dragons in the stories Mr. Ned used to tell him. Dan was so frightened that Scipio lifted him onto his wide shoulders and carried Dan into the train. He said, "Dan, be brave, you're the mascot now for Company E."

The trees, the cotton fields, the houses all whirled by until the train stopped at a place where there were rows of tents. Scipio told Dan it was called a bivouac area. "We'll drill here awhile," he said.

Dan watched the soldiers drill every day. Often he would creep behind a rock and see the cannoners fire round balls that burst in clouds of fire almost a mile away.

In the evening, around the campfires, the soldiers enjoyed listening to Li'l Dan play his drum.

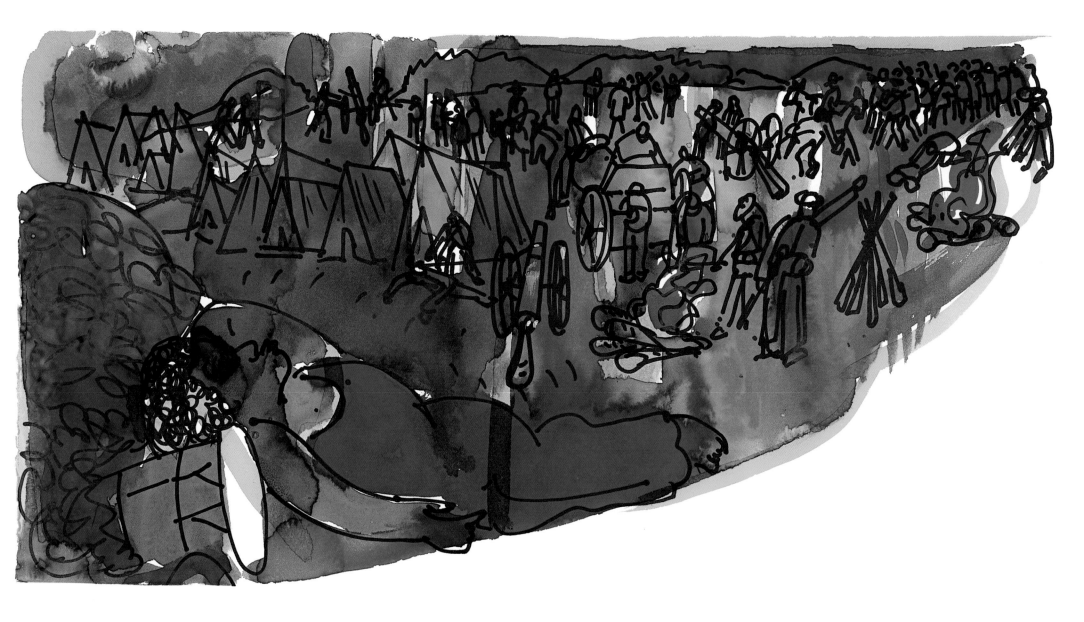

Very late one night the men were awakened by the sharp sound of the bugle. Some men shouted orders: "Everyone up! Fall in! Now . . . march!"

The men marched through the night. Dan ran along, but in the darkness no one noticed him.

By daybreak Dan saw his friends of Company E lined up. The woods ahead of them exploded with gunfire and cannon.

When Scipio saw Dan, he cried out: "Boy, you get away from here!
Go back over that hill and wait till we come for you!"

Dan climbed up a tree. He saw a long line of gray horsemen heading right to where **C**ompany **E** was posted—the same kind of men he had seen on the main road of the old plantation. **D**an knew **C**ompany **E** was in danger.

Dan wanted to do something, anything, to help his friends. **H**e could see the gray cavalry rushing toward him. **D**an had to act quickly. **H**e remembered the sound of the cannon at the camp.

an smacked the drum hard with his palms, but it wasn't the right sound. *Hurry! Hurry!* a voice inside him cried.

Dan broke off two sticks and hit the drum sharply with them. *Smack! Smack!* That's better! Just a bit sharper. *Crack! Crack!* Yes, this was it! This was the sound of the cannon the men called "five pounders."

The lead officer of the cavalry heard this sound. He raised his arm to halt the charge.

"Turn back, boys," he cried. "We're riding into a heap of cannon. We'll attack down that far road." With that the men in gray turned and galloped away.

The soldiers in Company E ran cheering toward Li'l Dan.

Big Scipio took Dan in his arms. "Dan," he said, "you and your drum surely saved us."

When the battle was over, General William T. Sherman himself asked to see Li'l Dan.

"Dan," the general said, "I learned of your heroism today—also what good use you made of that drum of yours. Now, Dan, I want you to be a drummer in our Army's Drum Corps. And listen, Dan, you play your drum in your own way."

And that's exactly what Li'l Dan did.